Ottoline and the Yellow Cat

Coming soon:

Ottoline Goes to School
Ottoline at Sea

Chris RIDDELL

Ottoline
and the
Yellow Cat

HarperCollins*Publishers*

For my daughter, Katy

Chapter One

Ottoline lived on the twenty-fourth floor of the Pepperpot Building. It was called the P. W. Huffledinck Tower; but it looked just like a pepper pot, so everyone called it the Pepperpot Building.

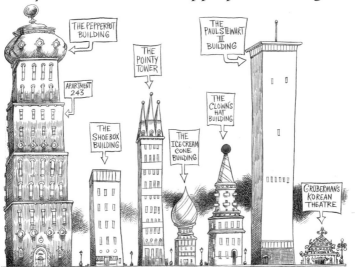

THE PEPPERPOT BUILDING

THE POINTY TOWER

THE PAUL STEWART III BUILDING

APARTMENT 243

THE CLOWN'S HAT BUILDING

THE SHOEBOX BUILDING

THE ICE CREAM CONE BUILDING

GRUBERMAN'S KOREAN THEATRE

LIKES SPLASHING IN PUDDLES AND COLLECTING THINGS

Ottoline

Mr. Munroe

SMALL, HAIRY, AND FROM A BOG IN NORWAY

She lived in apartment 243 with Mr. Munroe, who was small and hairy and didn't like the rain or having his hair brushed.

Ottoline, on the other hand, loved all kinds of weather, particularly rain, because she liked splashing in puddles. She also liked brushing Mr. Munroe's hair. She found it very relaxing, and it helped her to think, especially if there was a tricky problem to solve or a clever plan to work out.

Ottoline liked solving tricky problems and working out clever plans even more than she liked splashing in puddles. She kept her eyes and ears open in case she came across anything unusual or interesting. So did Mr. Munroe.

Ottoline's parents traveled the world collecting interesting things. Apartment 243 was full of the things that they collected.

EMPERORS' HATS

METEORITES

SEASHELLS

EXTREMELY SMALL PAINTINGS

SNUFF BOTTLES

HOT-WATER BOTTLES

BLUE BOTTLES

BUTTERFLY COLLECTORS' NETS

MASKS

PORTABLE FISHBOWLS

PARROT CLOCKS

LEAKING CUPS

Her parents had promised that one day, when she was older, Ottoline could join them on their travels, but until then she was to stay at home and look after their collections.

Ottoline didn't mind too much because she had Mr. Munroe for company.

MYSTERIOUS OBJECTS OF VARIOUS KINDS

One day, while out for an afternoon stroll, Mr. Munroe noticed a poster stuck to a lamppost outside Gruberman's Korean Theatre. He carefully peeled it off and folded it up. Then he put it under his arm, as, being small and hairy, Mr. Munroe didn't have any pockets. He took it home with him.

Later that afternoon, Ottoline was dusting
the four-spouted teapot collection when she
felt a tap on her shoulder. It was Mr. Munroe.
He showed her the poster from the lamppost
outside Gruberman's Korean Theatre.

lost

A Penangese lapdog
answers to the name
Rupert Pom-Pom Fluffy-Tail

Much missed by his loving owner

Large Reward

CONTACT: Mrs. Loretta Lloyd, Apartment 11112,
The Pointy Tower, 3rd St., B.C.

ARMPIT HAIR

"How interesting," Ottoline said. "You don't have any more of these by any chance?"

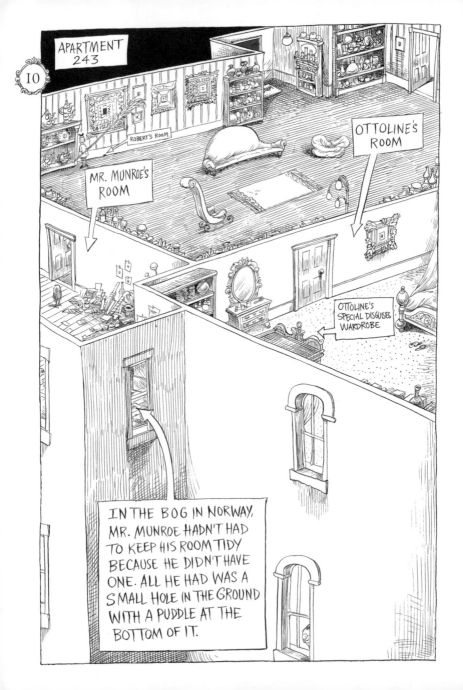

Mr. Munroe went to his room. It was very untidy.

When he came back, Ottoline was reorganizing her Odd Shoe collection.

Ottoline had two collections that were all her own. One was her Odd Shoe collection, of which she was very proud. Whenever Ottoline bought a pair of shoes, she would wear one and put the other in her collection.

IF YOU'D LIKE TO FIND OUT ABOUT OTTOLINE'S OTHER COLLECTION, TURN TO PAGE 45.

SOME OF OTTOLINE'S ODD SHOES

Mr. Munroe showed Ottoline the posters he'd collected from lampposts all over town.

Ottoline looked at them for a long time. "I don't suppose . . . ," she said, "you'd let me brush your hair?"

While she brushed Mr. Munroe's hair, Ottoline looked more closely at the posters.

THIS IS WHAT OTTOLINE LOOKS LIKE WHEN SHE'S THINKING OF A CLEVER PLAN.

WILSON HAPPY-EARS McMURTAGH

COUNT OLTO VIX-HILBURG

FIFI FIESTA FUNNY-FACE III

That evening Ottoline and Mr. Munroe sat
down to dinner. Ottoline had grilled cheese and
cinnamon toast freshly delivered to the table by

The Home-Cooked Meal Co. Mr. Munroe
had a bowl of porridge and a mug of hot
chocolate, which was the only meal he ever ate.

Happy Nest
BED MAKERS

THE
HOME-COOKED
MEAL Cº

OTTOLINE'S
PARENTS WERE
AWAY A LOT
TRAVELING, BUT
THEY MADE SURE
OTTOLINE
WAS WELL
LOOKED AFTER
BY LOTS AND
LOTS OF PEOPLE.
THESE ARE
THEIR BUSINESS
CARDS.

D.H.S.
Door Handle
Shiners
Inc.

MB
McBEAN'S CLEANING
SERVICE

Mr.
Munroe

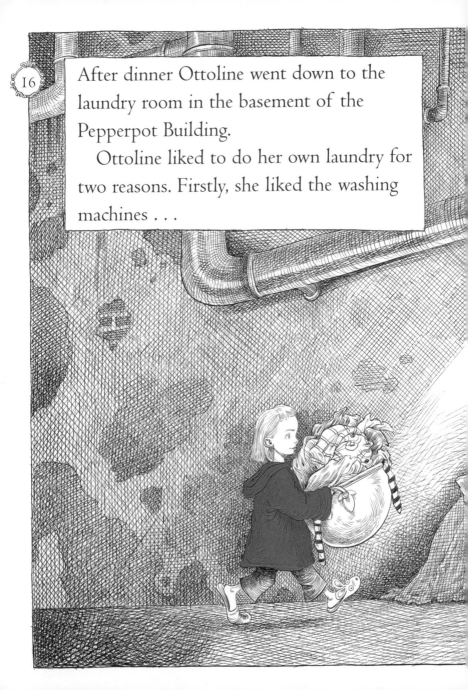

After dinner Ottoline went down to the
laundry room in the basement of the
Pepperpot Building.

Ottoline liked to do her own laundry for
two reasons. Firstly, she liked the washing
machines . . .

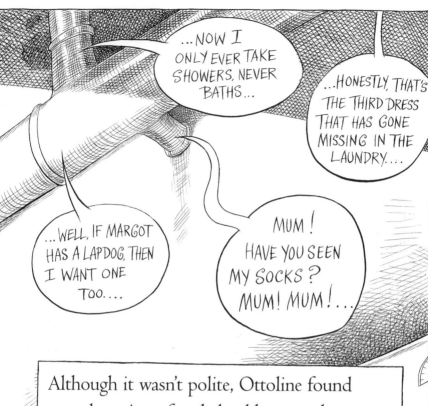

Although it wasn't polite, Ottoline found eavesdropping often helped her to solve tricky problems and think of clever plans.

It was Ottoline who found Mrs. Pasternak's missing monkey with a trail of honey-coated peanuts. And when the man from apartment 36 got his toe stuck in a tap, it was Ottoline who called the fire department.

That evening, Ottoline was doing her laundry
and listening to the pipes as usual when
a large, hairy arm appeared from behind
one of the washing machines and grabbed
a pair of Ottoline's stripy socks.

Ottoline peered into the shadows.

It was a bear.

"You ought to be ashamed of
yourself, stealing socks," said
Ottoline.

"So should you, listening
in on other people's
conversations," said
the bear.

"I won't tell
if you won't,"
said Ottoline.

Chapter Two

ROBERT IS IN THE HABIT OF READING OVER PEOPLE'S SHOULDERS.

MR. MUNROE IS IN THE HABIT OF DROPPING THE PAGES HE'S NOT INTERESTED IN ON THE FLOOR.

Mr. Munroe was sitting in the Beidermeyer armchair, reading the newspaper. Mr. Munroe often read his newspaper if he had trouble getting to sleep or had a bad dream about the bog in Norway. He liked to read the travel section, about vacations on tropical islands and sunny beaches.

Several pages caught Ottoline's eye.

ADVERTISING SECTION

CRIME SECTION

Ottoline got out a pair of Balinese pinking
shears from the scissors collection
and carefully cut out the arti-
cles. Mr. Munroe didn't
notice. He was engrossed
in a story about
the Gobi Desert,
where it hardly
ever rains.

IF YOU WOULD LIKE
TO SEE THIS PAGE
OF OTTOLINE'S NOTEBOOK, TURN THE PAGE.

NO NEW LEADS IN SHOE BOX BUILDING BURGLARY

By our crime correspondent

Police remain baffled by the burglary in the Shoe Box Building on 3rd Street. Despite extensive inquiries and prolonged investigations, Police Commissioner Ronald Flatfoot admitted, "We remain baffled." The victim of the burglary, Mrs. Rachel Armstrong, was too upset to talk to the *Enquirer* last night but said in a written statement, "I have nothing further to add." Police appealed to the public to be vigilant and on their guard at all times.

Mrs. Rachel Armstrong

*These dogs look strangely familiar

Mr. Munroe with a haircut!

BURGLARY AT THE POINTY TOWER BAFFLES POLICE

By our crime correspondent

Police remain baffled by the burglary at the Pointy Tower on Third Street. Despite extensive inquiries and prolonged investigations, Police Commissioner Ronald Flatfoot admitted, "We remain baffled." The victim of the burglary, Mrs. Dominica Wilson, was too outraged to talk to the *Enquirer* last night but said in a written statement, "I'm too outraged to talk." Police appealed to the public to be vigilant and on their guard at all times.

Mrs. Dominica Wilson

* Must investigate this ←

I wonder what has been nibbling my notebook? ↘

That night, after the Smith & Smith technicians had plumped the pillows and drawn the curtains, Ottoline got out of bed and went to her Special Disguises Wardrobe. Ottoline was a Mistress of Disguise and had a diploma to prove it, from the Who-R-U Academy of Subterfuge.

THIS IS THE DIPLOMA.

ACADEMY OF SUBTERFUGE

THIS IS TO CERTIFY THAT

Ottoline Brown

IS A CERTIFIED MISTRESS OF DISGUISE

PROFESSOR MYSTERY M.D.

When she was ready, she knocked on
Mr. Munroe's door.

"Your hair could do with a brush," said
Ottoline when he opened the door, "but we
haven't got time for that now. Here, put this
on." She handed Mr. Munroe a large, shabby
raincoat.

Mr. Munroe
handed her an
umbrella just
in case.

They set off through the city.

And very soon were . . .

. . . off the beaten track.

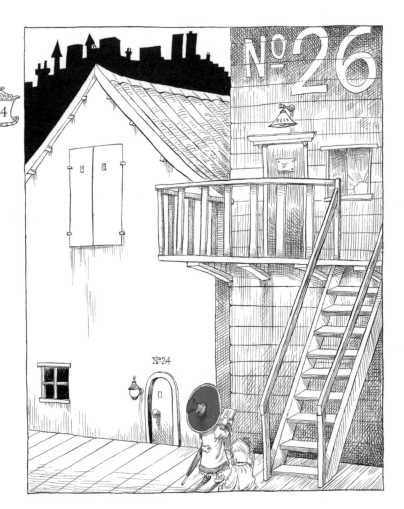

They came to an old warehouse.
Ottoline studied her notebook.

There was a sign on the door that read:

THE LAPDOG
AGENCY
——————————
BY APPOINTMENT
ONLY

Mr. Munroe was going to ring the bell,
but Ottoline stopped him. Instead they
looked through a rather grubby window.
This is what they saw. . . .

The poker players looked strangely familiar. Behind them, a cockatoo was talking into a telephone.

"I'm very sorry, madam, but that's company policy," the cockatoo was saying. "If you lose a lapdog we supplied you with, we can't trust you with another one, now can we? Good-bye."

The cockatoo put down the receiver.

Just then a yellow cat walked in.

"Good evening, boys," she purred. "Had a good week?"

The poker players wagged their tails.

"Excellent," purred the Yellow Cat. "Given Mrs. Neugerbauer the slip, I see, McMurtagh," she said, patting a small Lancashire terrier on the head.

"That's right, Boss," snarled the dog. "I ran out of the poodle parlor after one of those perfumed baths, and kept on running."

"Good work," said the Yellow Cat. "Now, boys, time for business. Show me what you've got."

The poker players put down their cards and picked up their pencils and started scribbling.

"Bring them to me, Clive!" said the Yellow Cat.

The cockatoo flapped about gathering up the drawings in his beak and took them to the Yellow Cat.

"Excellent," she purred.

THIS IS ONE OF THEM

my bed

Kitshun

Open Window

bed room

sitting room

Front door

Jewels

2880, Clown's hat Bilding

A Penangese lapdog dropped his doggy chew. "I ran off in the park this morning. Mrs. Lloyd threw me a stick, and she's still waiting for it. But I'm not going back!"

The Yellow Cat smiled. "If this information is correct, my furry friend," she purred, "then you won't have to!"

Chapter Three

The next morning Ottoline woke up rather later than usual. She put on her Mongolian dressing gown and, stifling a yawn, shuffled down the hallway.

There was a postcard on the doormat.

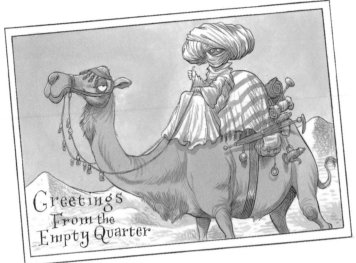

Greetings
From the
Empty Quarter

43

Dearest O, on the trail
of the most spectacular
camel hair coat to add
to our collection. Please
try not to spill jam down
the front of your mongolian
dressing gown, there's a dear.
The desert is very hot and it
never rains here. Mr. Munroe would
love it! Pa sends his love,
                              Ma
P.S. Remember to put the umbrella
back in the stand and don't
stay up too late tonight!
                    X X X

POSTCARD

EMPTY
E   4·02·07
QUARTER

Miss O. Brown,
Apt. 243,
The Pepperpot Bld.
3rd Street,
BIG CITY 3001

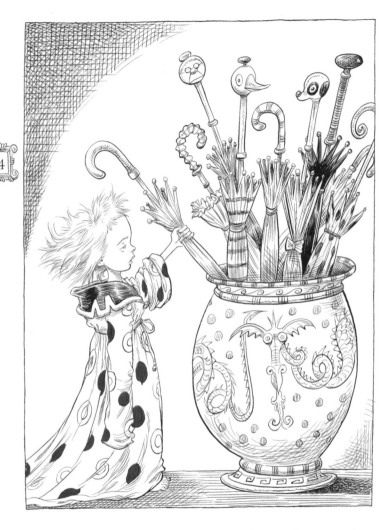

Ottoline put the umbrella back in the stand
and yawned sleepily.

Then she went to her room to put the postcard in her Postcard collection.

Ottoline loved her Postcard collection even more than her Odd Shoe collection. This was because all the postcards were from her parents.

Ottoline liked looking at the pictures of faraway places on the fronts of the postcards . . .

THIS IS OTTOLINE'S
SECOND COLLECTION

. . . and she loved reading the messages on the backs, because they made her feel as if her parents weren't so far away.

These are a few of her favorites:

Greetings
From the
Far East

Greetings
From the
Frozen
South

IF YOU WANT TO READ THE MESSAGES ON THE BACK, TURN THE PAGE. →

POSTCARD

Dearest O, Have never seen so many polar bears! The igloo we are staying in is very warm and snug. Please remember to shut the fridge door, there's a love. It's snowing again; don't think Mr. Monroe would like it here. Pa sends his love,
Ma
P.S. On your walks, make sure Mr. Monroe wraps up warm in Pa's raincoat. XXX

FROZEN ★ 13·04·05 ★ NORTH

6248

Miss O. Brown,
Apt. 243,
The Pepperpot Bld.
3rd Street,
BIG CITY 3001

POSTCARD

Dearest O, Finally we have found the Emperor of Heligoland's walking hat! Pa sends his love, lots of love,
Ma

P.S. Put the top back on the toothpaste!
X X X

WILD ★ 10·06·06 ★ WEST

4¢

Miss O. Brown,
Apt. 243,
The Pepperpot Bld.
3rd Street,
BIG CITY 3001

Postcard 1

POSTCARD

Dearest O, ran across some butterfly collectors in the jungle here. Pa was VERY CROSS and took away their butterfly collectors' nets! He sends his love,
Ma

P.S. Tidy your Odd Shoe collection, there's a good girl! XXX

FAR 9·11·05 EAST

Miss O. Brown,
Apt. 243,
The Pepperpot Bld.
3rd Street,
BIG CITY 3001

Postcard 2

POSTCARD

Dearest O, There are penguins everywhere! Emperor penguins, King Penguins and Vice-President penguins... The ship is frozen solid in the ice so we're stuck here for a bit. Don't forget to dust the four-spouted teapot collection, my darling.
Pa sends his love,
Ma

P.S. Well done! A diploma in disguise is a very useful thing to have.

FROZEN 29·07·06 SOUTH

88

Miss O. Brown,
Apt. 243,
The Pepperpot Bld.
3rd Street,
BIG CITY 3001

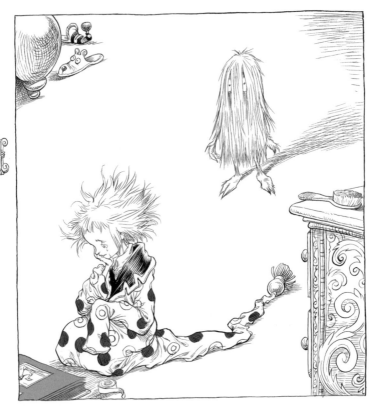

Ottoline was just putting the postcard in her
collection when Mr. Munroe walked in.
She showed him the postcard.

He looked at it for a long time and then
picked up Ottoline's hairbrush.

"My hair needs brushing?" asked Ottoline.

Mr. Munroe nodded. Next to having his own
hair brushed, the thing he liked least was
brushing someone else's. But he knew that it
would make Ottoline feel better, so he did
the best he could.

For breakfast that morning Ottoline
had strawberry bagels and apple juice.
Mr. Munroe had porridge and hot chocolate,

which he didn't touch because he was too
busy reading the newspaper.

"It's rude to read at the table," said Ottoline.

After breakfast, as they sat together on the Beidermeyer sofa, Mr. Munroe showed Ottoline something he had underlined in the newspaper in red crayon.

ROBERT FINISHED MR. MUNROE'S PORRIDGE FOR HIM, WHICH MADE HIM FEEL RATHER FULL

OTTOLINE LIKED TO CHANGE HER HAIRSTYLE EVERY DAY. ON TUESDAYS SHE GENERALLY WORE BRAIDS AND A BOW.

MR. MUNROE'S HAIRSTYLE NEVER CHANGED.

55

TO SEE WHAT MR. MUNROE UNDERLINED, TURN THE PAGE.

THE BIG CITY ENQUIRER

CAT BURGLAR STRIKES AGAIN

By our crime correspondent

Mrs. Loretta Lloyd

Mrs. Loretta Lloyd of the Clown's Hat Building on Third Street was the latest victim to fall prey to the "Notorious Cat Burglar." Mrs. Lloyd lost jewelry worth quite a lot in the robbery and was too angry to talk to the *Enquirer* last night but said in a written statement, "I'm so angry!" Police Commissioner Ronald Flatfoot admitted, "We are baffled," and appealed to the public to be vigilant and on their guard at all times.

"Mr. Munroe," said Ottoline, "I think it's time you practiced your Special Disguises."

Chapter Four

Just then the doorbell rang. Mr. Munroe went to the front door and opened it.

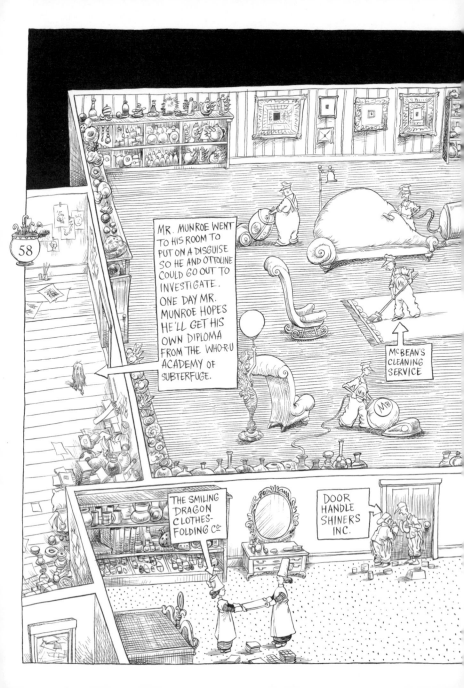

58

MR. MUNROE WENT TO HIS ROOM TO PUT ON A DISGUISE SO HE AND OTTOLINE COULD GO OUT TO INVESTIGATE. ONE DAY MR. MUNROE HOPES HE'LL GET HIS OWN DIPLOMA FROM THE WHO-R-U ACADEMY OF SUBTERFUGE.

McBEAN'S CLEANING SERVICE

THE SMILING DRAGON CLOTHES-FOLDING Co.

DOOR HANDLE SHINERS INC.

1,000-STRONG
LIGHTBULB-
CHANGING
Cº.

59

THE HOME-
COOKED
MEAL Cº.

OTTOLINE
LIKED TO
SUPERVISE

SMITH & SMITH
PILLOW-PLUMPING
AND CURTAIN-DRAWING
TECHNICIANS

MARION'S
BATHROOM
SUPPLIES

HAPPY NEST
BED
MAKERS

WELCOME

AT TEN O'CLOCK Mr. Munroe came out of
his room and tapped Ottoline on the
shoulder. He was wearing a large, shabby
raincoat.

Ottoline checked the curtains.

"Not now, Mr. Munroe," she said.

Mr. Munroe went back to his room.

AT ELEVEN O'CLOCK Mr. Munroe tapped
Ottoline on the shoulder again. He was
wearing a large, shabby raincoat and a pair
of dark glasses.

Ottoline looked at the door handle.

"Not now, Mr. Munroe," she said.

Mr. Munroe went back to his room.

AT TWELVE O'CLOCK Mr. Munroe coughed
loudly. He was wearing a large, shabby
raincoat, a pair of dark glasses and the
Emperor of Heligoland's hat.

Ottoline examined the toothpaste.

"Not now, Mr. Munroe," she said.

Mr. Munroe went back to his room and
slammed the door.

At lunch . . .

. . . there was very little conversation.

Mr. Munroe was wearing a large shabby rain-coat, a pair of dark glasses, the Emperor of Heligoland's hat and an extremely long scarf.

Ottoline inspected her knickers.

"Not now," she said.

AT FOUR O'CLOCK

"Not now," Ottoline said.

AT FIVE O'CLOCK

"Not now."

72

RIDDELL

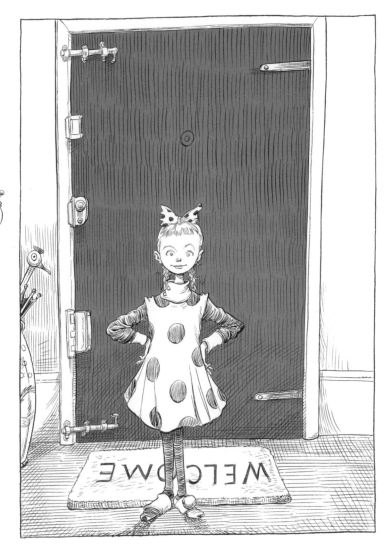

When everyone had gone, Ottoline closed the
front door and turned around.

"Now, Mr. Munroe," she said, "what is it . . . ?"

But Mr. Munroe wasn't there.

Chapter Five

Mr. Munroe
climbed up the
fire escape that
led to the roof of
the Pepperpot Building.
Every so often, he paused and
listened at the windows.
Mr. Munroe liked listening to the
interesting conversations that went on in
the other apartments. But he didn't tell
Ottoline, as he knew she wouldn't approve.

Mr. Munroe stood on the roof of the
Pepperpot Building and thought for a
long time.

It began to rain ...

. . . very heavily.

As he stood in the rain, Mr. Munroe thought about the cold, wet bog in Norway. He remembered how Ottoline's parents, Professor and Professor Brown, had found him and had invited him to come home with them to the Pepperpot Building.

Professor Brown lent him his nice new raincoat, and Professor Brown gave him her sunglasses. The three of them sailed home on the SS *Trondheim*. To avoid unwanted attention they called him Mr. Munroe, although his real name was something in Norwegian that meant "Small-Hairy-Bog-Person."

From the
moment she
was born,
Ottoline and
Mr. Munroe were
inseparable.

He took her for walks.

He let her brush his hair.

He even let her give him a bath . . .

. . . but only once.

But whatever they did, Ottoline's parents
knew that as long as Mr. Munroe was with
her, their daughter would always be safe.

The rain stopped, and Mr. Munroe went
down the fire escape. He didn't feel sad
any longer.

He stood on the doormat until he had
stopped dripping.

It felt good to be out of the rain. It felt
good to be far away from the bog in Norway.
It felt good to be living in
the Pepperpot
Building.

Most of all, it felt good to have Ottoline as
his best friend.

Mr. Munroe found Ottoline sitting in the Beidermeyer rocking chair.

OTTOLINE WAS MAKING NOTES IN HER NOTEBOOK.

MR. MUNROE KNEW HOW RELAXING OTTOLINE FOUND BRUSHING HIS HAIR, ESPECIALLY AFTER A BUSY DAY.

"Would you like me to brush your hair?" asked Ottoline.

Mr. Munroe nodded.

When she had finished, Ottoline looked at
Mr. Munroe for a long time. Then she looked
at her notebook.

"I've got a clever plan," she said.

Chapter
Six

Late that night, there was a knock on the door of the old warehouse.

"Go away!" yelled the Yellow Cat. "We're closed! Callers by appointment only!"

There was another knock on the door, followed by a rather feeble bark.

"All right, all right," complained the Yellow Cat. "Keep your tail on. I'm coming, I'm coming!"

The Yellow Cat opened the door. There was a small, hairy dog outside. The small, hairy dog handed the Yellow Cat a card.

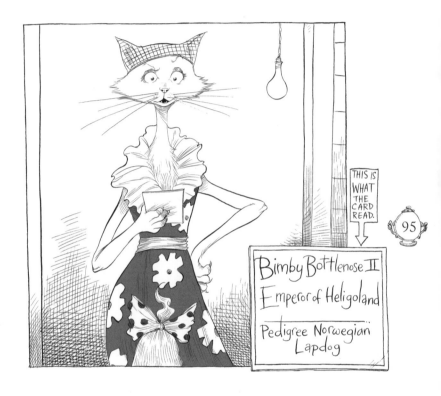

THIS IS WHAT THE CARD READ.

95

Bimby Bottlenose II
Emperor of Heligoland

Pedigree Norwegian
Lapdog

"Lapdog, eh?" said the Yellow Cat. "Then you've come to the right place!" She stepped aside and let him in.

"Look what the cat dragged in," said the Yellow Cat. "Boys, meet Bimby Bottlenose, Emperor of Heligoland."

The poker players looked up from their game.

"We can call him Nosy," said the Yellow Cat. "Nosy, meet the gang."

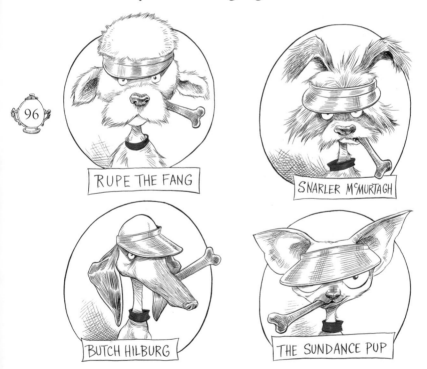

RUPE THE FANG

SNARLER M°MURTAGH

BUTCH HILBURG

THE SUNDANCE PUP

The gang wagged their tails and made room for Nosy at the table.

"Clive!" said the Yellow Cat. "Make sure the boys don't stay up too late. We've got work tomorrow."

"You're the boss, Boss," squawked the cockatoo.

"So where are you
from, stranger?" said
Rupe the Fang.
Nosy gave him his card.
Rupe looked at it.
"Norway," he said.
"It can get very wet
in Norway."
Nosy nodded and put a
playing card on the table.

"Emperor of Heligoland?"
said Butch Hilburg, chewing
on his doggy treat. "I once
saw the Emperor of
Heligoland. Wore a
splendid hat."

Nosy nodded
and played
another card.

"Care for a doggy treat?" offered
McMurtagh.

Nosy shook his head.

"Don't say much, do you?" McMurtagh
snarled. "What's wrong? Cat got your
tongue?"

"Don't mind him," said The Sundance Pup.
"He's just sore because his last owner took
him to the poodle parlor for a shampoo."

Nosy laid his playing cards on the table.

"Full house!" squawked Clive. "You win!
Time for bed!"

Nosy didn't sleep well in the lapdogs'
basket. Rupe the Fang snored, Snarler
McMurtagh whimpered, Butch Hilburg
chased squirrels in his dreams, and The
Sundance Pup
had terrible
gas.

He was just beginning to doze off when the
door opened and the Yellow Cat crept in.

The Yellow Cat opened her bag and
took out an emerald necklace, which
she carefully hid beneath the
floorboards.

Just then, the telephone rang.
The Yellow Cat leaped in the air with
surprise, and Clive woke up with a squawk.
"Don't just perch there!" hissed the Yellow
Cat. "Answer it."

Clive picked up the
receiver.

"The Lapdog Agency,
how may we help you?" he
said. "A lapdog? Certainly,
madam. We have an excellent
selection. Would you care to make
an appointment . . . this morning? . . . Yes,
I think we can fit you in. . . . What time? . . .
Now? Well, I suppose . . . Let me see. . . ."

Just then there was a
knock at the door.

"Must I do
EVERYTHING
myself?" said the
Yellow Cat,
slinking
up the
stairs.

103

Chapter Seven

The Yellow Cat opened the door. An extremely large lady was standing on the doorstep.

"Can I help you?" said the Yellow Cat.

"Mrs. Ursula Jansen-Smith," said the large lady grandly. "I am an incredibly rich but lonely old lady, and I'd like a lapdog to take home with me. I've just made an appointment."

Clive put down the telephone.

"Please come in, Mrs. Jansen-Smith," purred the Yellow Cat.

"You can call me Ursula," said the lady.

THE LAMPSHADE FROM PAGE 14

THE EXTREMELY LONG SCARF FROM PAGE 68

THE SUNGLASSES FROM PAGE 85

THE FUR COAT FROM PAGE 20

THE GLOVES FROM PAGE 70

105

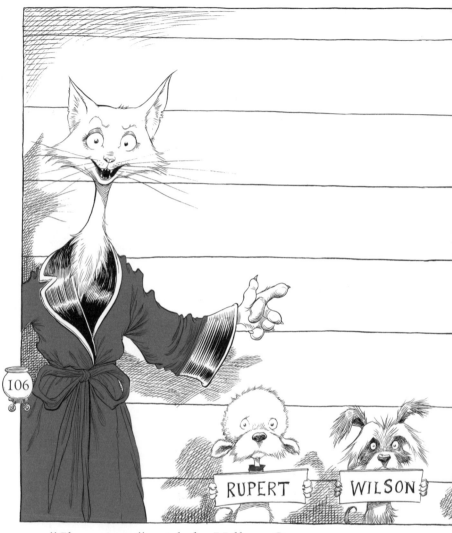

"Showtime!" said the Yellow Cat.

OLTO FIFI Bimby

The lapdogs lined up against the wall. They
held cards with their lapdog names on them.

Mrs. Jansen-Smith walked slowly down the
line and looked carefully at each lapdog.

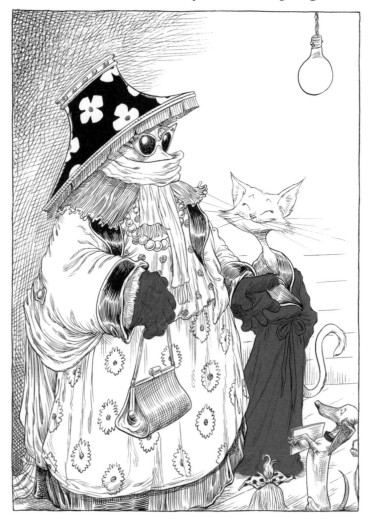

"Can I just say what an exquisite hat you're wearing, Mrs. Jansen-Smith?" purred the Yellow Cat, rubbing her paws. "And what a simply stunning outfit."

109

"My hat?" said Mrs. Jansen-Smith. "Do you like it? It was a present from the Emperor of Jutland. And these things? Oh, they're straight from the laundry. I just threw them together!"

Mrs. Jansen-Smith stopped in front of the
last lapdog.

"I'll take this one," she said.

"Excellent choice," purred the Yellow Cat.
"Bimby Bottlenose, Emperor of Heligoland,
is a pedigree Norwegian lapdog."

"It can get very wet in Norway," said Mrs.
Jansen-Smith thoughtfully. "Send me the
bill. Apartment 243, the Pepperpot Building,
Third Street."

III

When Mr. Munroe got back to apartment 243, he found a postcard on the doormat. He picked it up and went to see Ottoline. She was busy writing in her notebook.

Mr. Munroe handed her the postcard.

"Your ribbon has come undone," she said.

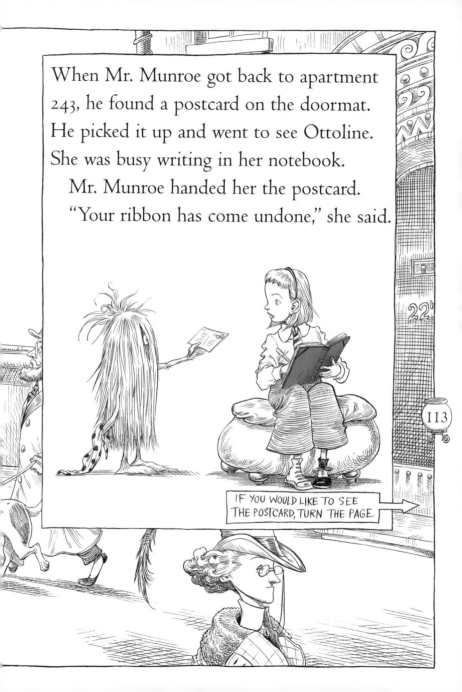

IF YOU WOULD LIKE TO SEE
THE POSTCARD, TURN THE PAGE.

THE TRONDHEIM UMBRELLA FESTIVAL

POSTCARD

Dearest O, Pa has
found some splendid
new umbrellas.

lots of love,
Ma
x x x

P.S. Make sure Mr.
Munroe gets to bed!
x x

TRONDHEIM
NORWAY
B. 28·4·07

Miss O. Brown,
Apt. 243,
The Pepperpot Building
3rd Street,
BIG CITY 3001

115

"It looks very wet, doesn't it, Mr. Munroe,"
said Ottoline. "Mr. Munroe . . . ?"

But Mr. Munroe was fast asleep.

117

Chapter Eight

The next morning, Mr. Munroe got up bright and early. He wandered around the apartment . . .

EMPERORS' HATS

EXTREMELY SMALL PAINTINGS

119

BUTTERFLY COLLECTORS' NETS

. . . making careful notes.

243

HOME-COOKED
CUSTARD PIE
HOME-COOKED
CUSTARD PIE
HOME-COOKED
CUSTARD PIE

OTTOLINE'S
BOLIVIAN LLAMA-
WOOL ROBE

The doorbell rang. Ottoline went to the front
door and opened it.

"We're not too early, I hope," said the chef
from The Home-Cooked Meal Company.

"No," said Ottoline. "There's lots to get
ready."

For breakfast, Ottoline had waffles and maple
syrup. Mr. Munroe had porridge and hot
chocolate, which he didn't touch because he
was busy finishing his notes.

"It's rude to write at the table," said
Ottoline.

After breakfast, as they sat on the Beidermeyer ottoman, Mr. Munroe showed Ottoline his notes.

She looked at them for a long time and then she said, "Good work, Mr. Munroe."

ROBERT CARRYING A PIECE OF LEFTOVER WAFFLE

Then Ottoline brushed Mr. Munroe's hair . . .

. . . very
thoroughly . . .

. . . and tied a ribbon in it.

She kissed him on the forehead.

"You're very brave," she said. "Now you'd better go."

Mr. Munroe nodded.

Ottoline waited until Mr. Munroe had gone,
and then she walked to Gruberman's Korean
Theatre. She carefully unfolded a poster and
stuck it to the lamppost.

LOST

A Pedigree Norwegian
Lapdog
answers to the name of
Bimby Bottlenose II
Emperor of Heligoland
much missed by his loving owner
LARGE REWARD
Contact Mrs. Jansen-Smith Apartment 243
THE PEPPERPOT BUILDING · 3rd Street · B.C.

129

Mr. Munroe knocked on the warehouse door.

"Hiya, Nosy," the Yellow Cat said. "You're a fast worker."

REPAIRED
BUTTERFLY
COLLECTOR'S
NET

133

IF YOU WOULD LIKE TO
SEE THE PIECE OF PAPER,
TURN THE PAGE.

The gang crowded round.

"OK, show me what you've got," said the
Yellow Cat.

Nosy handed her a piece of paper.

Apartment 243, the Pepperpot Building

↑ Emperors' hats

extremely small paintings

sofa

NOTHING interesting HERE!

← rocking Chair

← Collections

armchair

← dressing table

↑ odd shoe collection

Fire Escape

← Wardrobe

Window

Mrs. Jansen-Smith's Bedroom

Window

front door

Umbrellas

WELCOME

Collections↗

Dining

Sitting room

↙Ottoman

↘collections

↙collections

room

Kitchen

Pots →

bed →

bathroom

135

window

✗ Jewels are in this closet

ARMPIT HAIR

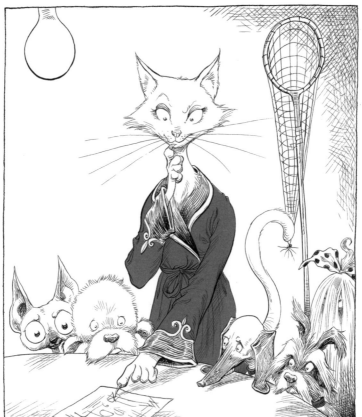

The Yellow Cat looked at the drawing for
a long time. "Excellent work, Nosy," she
purred as she left the room. "Excellent."

"Welcome back," snarled Snarler
McMurtagh. "Feeling lucky?"

Nosy nodded and sat down at the table with the other lapdogs. Butch Hilburg dealt the cards.

"Didn't take you long to give your owner the slip," said Rupe the Fang. "Very careless, some of these ladies."

Nosy nodded again and played a card.

"So is the rumor true?" Butch said to Rupe. "Are you thinking of going back to Mrs. Lloyd?"

"What if I am?" replied Rupe. "Sometimes a dog just wants a quiet lap to sit on for the rest of his days. I'm getting too old for a life on the run."

"I miss Mrs. Armstrong," said The Sundance Pup with a sniff.

Nosy put his last card on the table.

"Full house!" squawked Clive the cockatoo. "You win!"

Chapter Nine

That night, as the lapdogs slept in their basket, the Yellow Cat tiptoed up the stairs and out of the door without a sound.

Butch Hilburg turned over and thumped his tail, and Rupe the Fang licked his chops noisily and got comfortable before he started snoring again.

Mr. Munroe
gently
removed
Snarler
McMurtagh's
front paws from
his head and
quietly climbed
out of the basket.
Reaching up, he tugged his
bow undone and let the ribbon fall to
the floor. Then he tiptoed across to the
corner of the room.

Mr. Munroe carefully
tilted the loose floor-
board. It gave a
small creak.

140

141

Clive woke up and saw Mr. Munroe with
the loot. He let out a piercing screech:
"Stop, thief!"

But Mr. Munroe
was prepared.

He tied up Clive firmly with the polka-dot
ribbon, wrapping it once around his legs,
twice around his wings, and three times
around his beak. He then tied a bow in it and
pulled it tight.

"Umph! Umph! Umph!" said Clive.

Mr. Munroe then sat down at the table,
picked up the telephone, and started to dial. . . .

Just then the doorbell rang, and the lapdogs woke up.

"What time is it?" snarled Snarler McMurtagh.

"I was having a wonderful dream about squirrels," yawned Butch Hilburg.

"What's that terrible smell?" asked The Sundance Pup.

"Umph! Umph! Umph!" said Clive the cockatoo.

The doorbell rang again.

Mr. Munroe climbed the stairs and opened
the door.

Four ladies came in. They looked strangely familiar.

Mr. Munroe presented each of them with their stolen jewels.

"Time to come home, you naughty, naughty boy," said Mrs. Armstrong.

The Sundance Pup wagged his tail.

"Walkies!" said Mrs. Lloyd.

Rupe the Fang barked excitedly.

"Here, boy!" said Mrs. Wilson, and Butch Hilburg rushed up to her.

"Come to Mummy!" cooed Pinky Neugerbauer. "My little poodle-doodle!"

151

"You'll never take me alive!" snarled Snarler McMurtagh.

The ladies thanked Mr. Munroe
for all his help. They promised
not to press charges as long as
the lapdogs behaved
themselves.

155

When they had gone, Mr. Munroe locked the
door of the old warehouse.

Then he picked up Clive the cockatoo and
set off toward the Pepperpot Building.

Chapter Ten

The Yellow Cat climbed in through the window of apartment 243 and looked around.

With one gloved paw, she reached into her bag and took out Mr. Munroe's drawing. She examined it carefully, then crept on tiptoe toward Ottoline's bedroom.

pening the door a crack, the Yellow Cat pped inside. She didn't make a sound.

hen she sneaked over to the closet and owly opened it. . . .

closet

Happy
nest
bed
makers

bed

pots

smiling
dragon
co.

1000-strong
co.

Smith
+
Smith

Home-
cooked
meal c⁰

Door
Handle
Shiners

McBean's
Cleaners

Bedroom
Plan

Y.C.

Marion's
Bathroom
supplies

Fire Escape

OTTOLINE'S
NOTEBOOK

Suddenly a light flicked on.

With a startled meow the Yellow Cat sprang to her feet and dashed for the door.

Dodging a collapsing tower of neatly folded nightgowns . . .

ducking an avalanche of perfectly plumped pillows . . .

. . . she leaped over the vacuum cleaner and
the floor mop . . .

. . . and swerved under the swishing shower
curtain.

The Yellow Cat struggled to get a grip on the shiny doorknob. She was about to try for the window when . . .

. . . half a dozen home-cooked custard pies sailed through the air toward her . . .

. . . and an incredibly large bear jumped out
of the neatly made bed.

"Mrs. Jansen-Smith!" yowled the Yellow
Cat.

The bear caught her in a big bear hug.
"Curses!" hissed the Yellow Cat.

"Hello," said Ottoline. "You didn't really think you'd get away with it, did you?"

"Tell me, how did you do it?" asked the Yellow Cat.

"Simple – with the help of my friends," said Ottoline, "and a clever plan."

OTTOLINE'S MADAGASCAN MOHAIR DRESSING GOWN →

Just then the doorbell rang.

It was Mr. Munroe and the pet police.

"We'll take it from here, miss," said the pet policeman to Ottoline. "We've been after these two for quite a while."

"What will happen to them?" asked Ottoline.

"They'll be going away for a very long time," said the policeman. "To a petting zoo in the country."

"Curses!" said Clive the cockatoo.

Ottoline turned to Mr. Munroe and gave him a hug. "I'm very, very proud of you," she said.

Mr. Munroe nodded and Ottoline, who knew Mr. Munroe better than anyone else in the world, was sure that he was smiling.

167

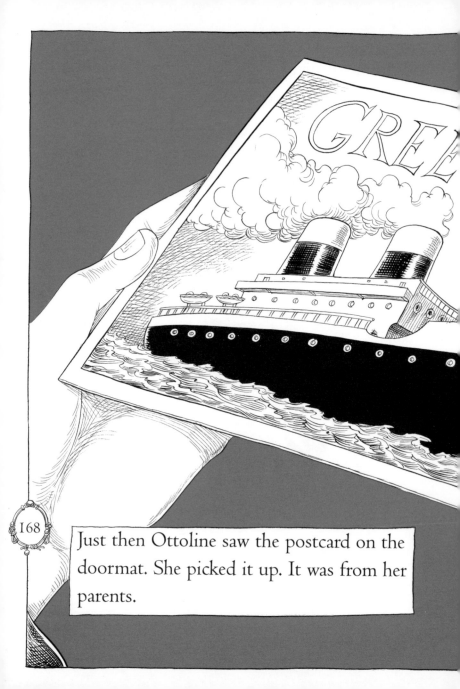

Just then Ottoline saw the postcard on the doormat. She picked it up. It was from her parents.

Dearest O,

we are on our way home. Pa and I can't wait to see you,

lots of love,

Ma

P.S. Tell that nice bear he can stay as long as he wants.

P.P.S. Please clear up those custard pies, there's a good girl! XXX

Miss O. Brown,
Apartment 243,
The Pepperpot Bld.
3rd Street,
BIG CITY 3001

ACADEMY OF SUBTERFUGE

THIS IS TO CERTIFY THAT

Mr. Munroe

IS A CERTIFIED MASTER OF
DISGUISE

PROFESSOR MYSTERY
M.D.

Bowen Press is an imprint of HarperCollins Publishers.

Ottoline and the Yellow Cat
Copyright © 2007 by Chris Riddell
All rights reserved.
Manufactured in China.

Library of Congress Control Number: 2007934947
ISBN 978-0-06-144881-2
09 10 11 12 13 SCP 10 9 8 7 6 5 4 3 2 1
❖
First American Edition, 2008
Originally published in Great Britain in 2007 by Macmillan Children's Books